D1571339

Book 3: VISION of a STAR

CLAIRVOYANT CLAIRE

Spellbound

An Imprint of Magic Wagon
abdobooks.com

BY JENNY SCOTT   ILLUSTRATED BY BILLY YONG

FOR GAVIN AND BELLA -JS

TO RACHEL, FOR ALWAYS BELIEVING IN ME -BY

abdobooks.com

Published by Magic Wagon, a division of ABDO, PO Box 398166, Minneapolis, Minnesota 55439. Copyright © 2020 by Abdo Consulting Group, Inc. International copyrights reserved in all countries. No part of this book may be reproduced in any form without written permission from the publisher. Spellbound™ is a trademark and logo of Magic Wagon.

Printed in the United States of America, North Mankato, Minnesota.

102019
012020

Written by Jenny Scott
Illustrated by Billy Yong
Edited by Tamara L. Britton
Art Directed by Christina Doffing

Library of Congress Control Number: 2019942379

Publisher's Cataloging-in-Publication Data

Names: Scott, Jenny, author. | Yong, Billy, illustrator.
Title: Vision of a star / by Jenny Scott ; illustrated by Billy Yong.
Description: Minneapolis, Minnesota : Magic Wagon, 2020. | Series: Clairvoyant Claire; book 3
Summary: Twelve-year-old Olivia is psychic! In her latest vision, she sees a local theater star go missing right before her last performance. Olivia and her friend Sebastian warn the community on their blog Clairvoyant Claire. The public finally believes Clairvoyant Claire when the actor is found.
Identifiers: ISBN 9781532136580 (lib. bdg.) | ISBN 9781532137181 (ebook) | ISBN 9781532137488 (Read-to-Me ebook)
Subjects: LCSH: Clairvoyants--Juvenile fiction. | Blogs--Juvenile fiction. | Stage actors--Juvenile fiction. | Kidnapping--Juvenile fiction. | Mystery and detective stories--Juvenile fiction. | Friendship--Juvenile fiction. | Self-confidence--Juvenile fiction.
Classification: DDC [Fic]--dc23

Table of Contents

CHAPTER 1
A Star in Trouble

I jolt upright in bed. A VISION zips into my head and my arms prickle with GOOSE BUMPS.

I'm on stage at the local theater. The star of the play rehearses her lines. She's wearing a *gauzy* white dress and a crown of flowers.

All of a sudden, the lights go out.

Someone screams.

When the **LIGHTS** come back on, the star is gone.

The VISION clears like a **FOG** and I look around my bedroom. The clock says it's only 5:00 a.m., but no way will I be able to **SLEEP** after that.

I **TIPTOE** out of bed and my goldendoodle puppy, Rocky, follows me downstairs. I start the computer while Rocky *curls* up at my feet. In a new search window, I type in Edgewood Theater and **CLICK** on the first result.

On the **FRONT** page of the theater's website is a poster for the **NEW** production of *A Midsummer Night's Dream*. I recognize the girl on the poster from my VISION.

Her *name* is Lola Kinsey. She's playing Hermia, one of the LEAD roles. The website says the last performance is tonight.

I **GRAB** the phone and call my friend Sebastian.

"Olivia?" he says groggily. "It's still **dark** out!"

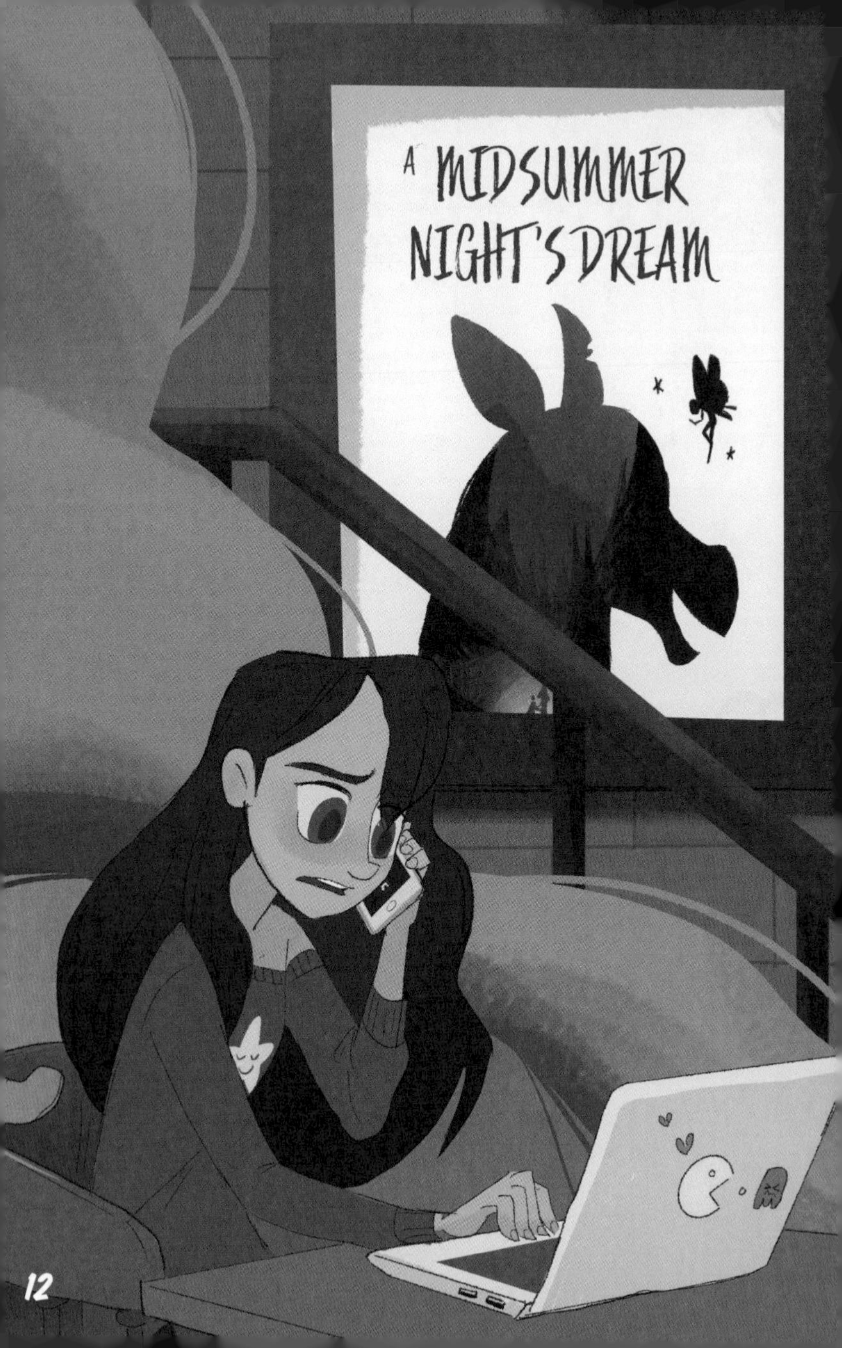
A MIDSUMMER NIGHT'S DREAM

"I had a VISION."

"And it couldn't wait?"

"Lola Kinsey is going to disappear from the stage tonight before the last production of *A Midsummer Night's Dream*. We have to post a **WARNING** on Clairvoyant Claire's blog to warn her, so get up. I'll start making chocolate milk and waffles."

He **GROANS** but I can hear his bed squeaking as he climbs out of it. "Fine," he says. "I'll be there in ten minutes."

CHAPTER 2

The Show Must Go On

Sebastian barely speaks until he's *gobbled* up two waffles drenched in syrup and butter. "That's better," he says and **pats** his belly. Rocky *whines* at his feet. "Sorry, boy. I didn't save any for you."

"Rocky has kibble," I say. Sebastian SCRATCHES Rocky behind the ears. "I know and I feel terrible for him."

Once the breakfast dishes are in the dishwasher, we go back to the computer. Sebastian, the **FASTER** typer and the *Clairvoyant Claire* blog's tech WIZ, types while I speak.

CLAIRVOYANT CLAIRE

Dear Citizens of Edgewood,

TROUBLE is coming

to the Edgewood Theater

before ~~tonight's~~ show. Lola

Kinsey, the play's star, may be

in **DANGER**. Please

shut down production to keep her

out of harm's way!

Sincerely, Clairvoyant Claire

FUJI

EDGEWOOD THEATER
PRESENTS

A MIDSUMMER NIGHT'S DREAM

FEATURING. LOLA KINSEY

SEPT 18 - 30, 2020

EDGEWOOD THEATER

idsummer Night's Dream

s Now Available

"I have met Lola," Sebastian says once the post is *LIVE*. "I don't think she'll listen to us. She takes her CRAFT very seriously."

"I was afraid of that."

Since it's still early, Sebastian and I take Rocky for a WALK. When we return an hour later, there are a few NEW comments on the post.

Someone has tagged Lola Kinsey,
just as I'd hoped.

But Lola's reply says,

Clairvoyant Claire said I may be in **DANGER**. I'm confident the crew at Edgewood Theater will keep me **SAFE**. And my *wonderful* understudy Samantha is always ready to take the stage. The **SHOW** must go on!

CHAPTER 3
A Star Goes Dark

The **SHOW** is scheduled to begin at 7:00 p.m. so Sebastian and I **ARRIVE** at the theater a couple of hours before. Better to be early than late.

We **SLIP** in through a side door and run into Officer Ezra.

"Hello Olivia. Sebastian." Officer Ezra *rests* her hands on her duty belt. "What brings you two here? The **SHOW** is still *HOURS* away."

Sebastian says, "Oh, we're just really excited!"

Officer Ezra **turns** to me. "Do either of you know about Clairvoyant Claire's NEW post? How is Lola in danger?"

"We don't know Claire," Sebastian says with a **NERVOUS** laugh.

Officer Ezra and I stare at each other with a certain kind of understanding. Suddenly, there's a **SCREAM** from inside the theater.

31

Officer Ezra **pushes** through the door. Sebastian and I follow behind and STUMBLE into complete **darkness**.

People are shouting to get the **LIGHTS** on. Someone yells, "Clairvoyant Claire was right! Lola! Are you okay?"

But Lola does **NOT** answer.

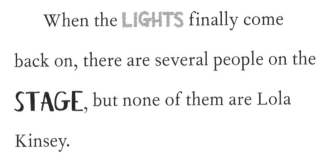

When the LIGHTS finally come back on, there are several people on the STAGE, but none of them are Lola Kinsey.

Officer Ezra turns to me. "I need Clairvoyant Claire's help."

CHAPTER 4
New Vision

We RUSH backstage and find Lola's dressing room. There's no one inside.

"Stay here while I *check* the other rooms," Officer Ezra says. "If you can make that POWER of yours work, now is the time!"

"It's not a **POWER**!" I yell but Officer Ezra is already gone.

Sebastian starts to **PACE**.

"Officer Ezra knows you're Claire!"

"I think she's known for a while." I search through Lola's possessions **LOOKING** for clues.

"Was there anything else in your VISION that might help?" Sebastian asks.

"All I saw was the stage." I grab Lola's hairbrush and ZAP. I get a chilly premonition of someone opening a **trapdoor** in the stage and Lola falling through it. When I SNAP out of it, I start for the door. "How do we get BENEATH the stage?"

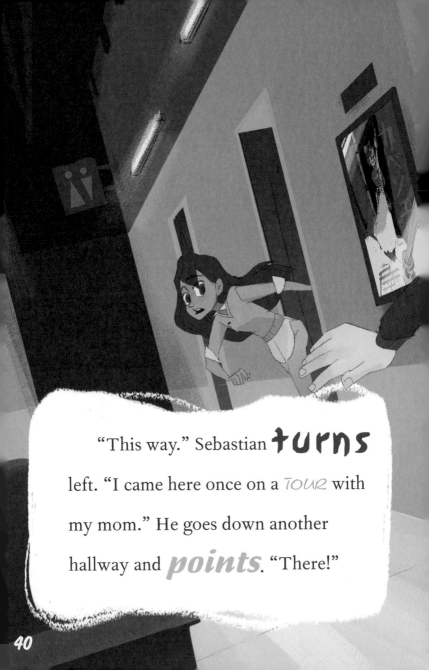

"This way." Sebastian **turns** left. "I came here once on a *TOUR* with my mom." He goes down another hallway and *points*. "There!"

We burst through the narrow door. It's MURKY inside, but we can see Lola tied to a chair and another girl standing OVER her. "I've been your understudy for too long," the girl says. "It's my time to SHINE!"

"Not QUITE." Officer Ezra comes up BEHIND them. "Put your hands on your head, Samantha."

"No!" Samantha *darts* for a second door, but Lola sticks her foot out and TRIPS her. Officer Ezra moves **QUICKLY** and within seconds, has Samantha handcuffed.

"It's not FAIR!" Samantha says. "Lola gets all of the **good** parts!"

"That's because Lola is **good**," Sebastian says.

Later, once Lola is **SAFE** and Samantha is off to **jail**, Officer Ezra takes me aside.

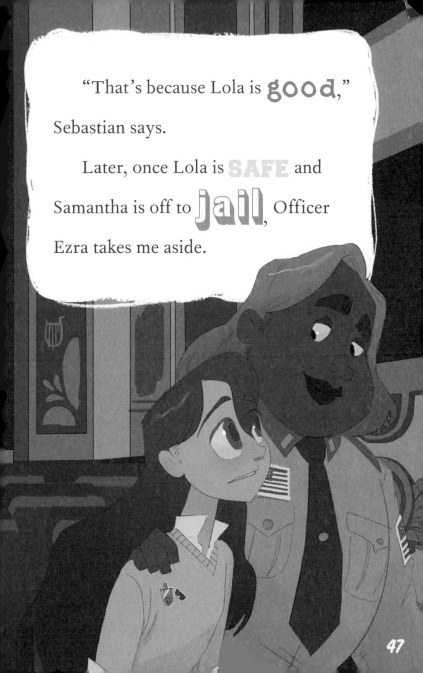

"Clairvoyant Claire, I **presume**?" she says.

"At your *service*, ma'am."

We **SHAKE** hands and smile.